D1505634

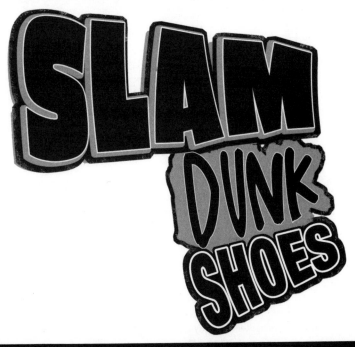

BY JAKE MADDOX

illustrated by Sean Tiffany

text by Bob Temple

Librarian Reviewer
Chris Kreie
Media Specialist, Eden Prairie Schools, MN
MS in Information Media, St. Cloud State University, MN

Reading Consultant
Mary Evenson
Middle School Teacher, Edina Public Schools, MN
MA in Education, University of Minnesota

▼▼ STONE ARCH BOOKS
Minneapolis   San Diego

Jake Maddox Books are published by Stone Arch Books,
A Capstone Imprint
1710 Roe Crest Drive
North Mankato, Minnesota 56003
www.capstonepub.com

Library of Congress Cataloging-in-Publication Data
Maddox, Jake.
    Slam Dunk Shoes / by Jake Maddox; illustrated by Sean Tiffany.
    p. cm. — (A Jake Maddox Sports Story)
    Summary: When Jamal is asked to join the elite Cyclone basketball
team, he worries that his ratty old shoes—all his family can afford—will
hurt his image on the team.
    ISBN-13: 978-1-59889-842-2 (library binding)
    ISBN-10: 1-59889-842-6 (library binding)
    ISBN-13: 978-1-59889-894-1 (paperback)
    ISBN-10: 1-59889-894-9 (paperback)
    [1. Basketball—Fiction. 2. Self-confidence—Fiction. 3. African
Americans—Fiction.] I. Tiffany, Sean, ill. II. Title.
PZ7.M25643Slm 2008
[Fic]—dc22   2007003633

Art Director: Heather Kindseth
Graphic Designer: Kay Fraser

Printed in the United States of America in Stevens Point, Wisconsin.
022013
007197R

TABLE OF CONTENTS

Chapter 1

Playground Legend

Jamal stooped low in his defensive crouch. The boy he was guarding stood tall before him, dribbling the ball back and forth between his legs. Back and forth, back and forth, the ball went.

Jamal watched it rock.

Finally, he couldn't take it anymore.

Jamal lunged for the ball. He tried to swipe it from the boy in mid-dribble.

It was just what the boy hoped Jamal would do. The boy pulled the ball back, swung it around his back, and started to drive quickly toward the basket.

Straight down the lane he went, leaving Jamal behind. But Jamal wasn't done. His tattered shoes pivoted on the blacktop, and Jamal made a beeline for the rim.

The boy was quick, but Jamal was quicker. Just as the layup went toward the hoop, Jamal jumped and got his finger on the ball.

The ball bounced off the backboard and landed squarely in the hands of one of Jamal's teammates.

By the time anyone could react, Jamal was already on his way down toward the other end of the court.

Jamal's teammate fired the ball toward midcourt. Jamal caught the ball easily. Then he sprinted toward the other basket.

Going straight to the hoop without a hint of showboating, Jamal pushed to the rim. He laid the ball up neatly off the backboard, and heard the clang as it dropped through the chain net.

"Two more!" yelled Michael, one of Jamal's friends.

Jamal just smiled. The other players were amazed at Jamal's speed, but they were not surprised by it.

After all, they had seen him make many incredible plays on the blacktop courts at Princeton Park. Even though he was only thirteen, Jamal was becoming a playground legend.

The game went on. Jamal was in control the whole way. The boy he was guarding managed to get free. He scored a couple of baskets, but Jamal always answered at the other end.

Jamal would drive the lane and toss a nifty pass to a wide-open teammate. He would slash to the rim for one of his perfect layups. Or he'd step back behind the three-point line and drop in a long jump shot.

After each shot, Michael would yell something from the sidelines. Jamal was never one to talk trash on the court. Michael wasn't quite as shy.

Pickup basketball games at the playground were always played up to twenty-one points.

Jamal's team led, 19–7.

Jamal finished the game off by stealing a pass.

Then he took the ball the length of the court for an easy basket.

When the ball dropped through the hoop, it was nearly dark outside.

"Time to head home," Jamal said.

His teammates slapped hands with each other. A few of them patted Jamal on the back.

Before long, he was making the eight-block walk through the streets to his apartment building.

Michael, who lived just a few floors below Jamal, walked along with him.

"So, what did he say?" Michael asked.

"What did who say?" Jamal responded.

"Your dad, man," Michael said. "What did he say about the shoes?"

Jamal knew what Michael was talking about now.

Jamal had been bugging his father for a special pair of basketball shoes.

They were called Show-25s. They were named after Jamal's favorite pro player, Kenny "The Show" Milton. Kenny Milton wore number 25.

There was only one thing wrong with the Show-25s: They cost more than a hundred dollars.

Jamal always hoped that one day he'd play on a real team, wearing top-of-the-line shoes, and wearing number 25.

Jamal glanced down at the tattered basketball shoes on his feet.

Once white, they were now covered with black marks from the court and dirt. Worse, they weren't even his. They were hand-me-downs from his older brother.

Finally, Jamal replied. "We can't afford them right now," he said.

Michael nodded.

Chapter 2

A New Opportunity

The next morning, Jamal met Michael and they walked together to school.

Michael was bubbling with excitement. Jamal wasn't sure why.

"What's up with you?" Jamal finally said.

Michael bounced down the sidewalk. "I got some news for you, man," Michael said. "Did you hear about the Cyclones?"

"The Cyclones?" Jamal responded. The Cyclones were the best youth team in the entire city. "What about them?"

"Yeah," Michael said. "I guess they are having tryouts."

"So what?" Jamal said. "None of us could ever make that team. It's the best team in the entire city. They have the same kids on that team every year."

"All they have to do is see you play, man," Michael said. "They'll have to take you."

"I don't think so," Jamal replied.

The boys walked the rest of the way in silence. But Jamal's mind was working overtime. All day at school, he thought about the tryouts for the Cyclones team. He couldn't get it out of his head.

At the same time, Jamal knew that his chances of making that team weren't very good.

The boys on the Cyclones had the best of everything: the best uniforms, the best gyms, the best shoes. They even had bright red warm-up jackets and pants to wear before their games.

Most of their parents had enough money for them to travel all over the area playing games every weekend.

Jamal's life was totally different from the Cyclone players'. He might be able to compete with them on the court, but not off of it.

After school, Jamal and Michael walked over to the playground to play some basketball.

When they arrived, there were already a bunch of high school players on the court. "We got next!" Michael declared. A couple of them smirked.

Soon, three other high school guys showed up.

"You boys looking to play some ball?" one of them said.

Michael perked right up. "Oh, yeah!" he said. "We're ready."

Jamal knew the older boys. He just smiled at them and tapped fists.

As always, Jamal was quiet on the court. But he was fixing his sights on the players. He was studying them quietly, trying to learn their weaknesses. By the time that game ended, Jamal felt ready to take on the winners.

Finally, one player lofted a soft shot from the lane that clinked through the chain-link net, ending the game.

Michael popped up right away and started gabbing. "Is that all you've got?" he barked at the older players.

"Better watch your mouth, small man," one of the boys shot back. Michael settled down a bit.

Jamal calmly walked out onto the court. He felt more comfortable there than any other place in the world.

Just before his game was about to start, Jamal saw something that made him a little nervous. A tall man was standing at the end of the court, holding a clipboard. He was wearing a bright red warm-up jacket.

Chapter 3

Surprise Visit

Jamal felt the butterflies flapping around in his stomach. For the first time ever, he was nervous on a basketball court.

"Hey, Jamal," Michael said. "Do you see what I see?"

"Yeah, Michael, I do," Jamal said. He was trying not to sound nervous.

"Looks like you don't have to try out for the Cyclones," Michael said. "Looks like your tryout is right now!"

Jamal just shook his head. It was time to play. Time to focus.

The other team was all high school boys, so Jamal and Michael would both have to guard much older players.

That never bothered Jamal. He liked playing against the older guys anyway. Even though he wasn't very tall, Jamal was quick.

Jamal matched up with a boy named Joseph. He was one of the better players at the high school.

Since Joseph's team won the previous game, they had control of the court.

As a result, they got to start with the ball first.

Joseph was a good ball handler, so he brought the ball up the court.

Jamal dropped down into his defensive crouch to guard him.

Joseph moved the ball to the right and fired a pass to a teammate. Then he cut behind Jamal and headed toward the basket. The return pass hit Joseph square in the hands, and he made an easy layup.

Jamal's heart sank. He had been burned by an easy play. That kind of play never worked on him. Did the Cyclones' coach notice? Was he already writing Jamal off as a player?

Michael grabbed the ball and passed it to Jamal. As soon as he had the ball in his hands, Jamal relaxed. He felt comfortable. He took the ball up the court, flipping it between his legs once or twice along the way.

When he crossed half-court, Jamal made eye contact with the biggest boy on his team.

The boy knew exactly what that meant. He cut along the baseline toward the basket and Jamal moved to his right with the ball.

Without looking, Jamal fired a one-handed pass up toward the rim. The boy leaped for it and slammed it down into the basket!

"Woooo!" Michael cried. "Try a little taste of that!"

Jamal smiled. The play had tied the score at 2–2. Jamal was feeling confident again.

The rest of the game went very well.

Jamal and Joseph played about evenly.

They each scored a few baskets and set up their teammates with some great passes. Joseph's team won the game.

Jamal had to sit a game out. When his team got back on the court, however, Jamal began to take charge.

The boys played for an hour or so. Finally, it was time to head home.

Before Jamal could get too far, however, the man in the red Cyclones jacket approached him.

"Excuse me," the man said. "Your name is Jamal, right?"

"Yes sir," Jamal replied quietly.

Michael wasn't so quiet. "That's right, he's Jamal," Michael shouted. "And he's the man!"

The Cyclones coach laughed. "I'm Coach Barker. You're a good player," he said to Jamal. "You'd look awfully good in a Cyclones uniform."

Jamal smiled. "Are you serious?" he said. "Me?"

"Yes, you," the coach said. "If you're interested, you'd need to come to a practice to see how you stack up against our players. Talk it over with your mom or dad. If you're interested, we'll see you on Saturday."

Chapter 4

Show-25s

Jamal rushed home to talk to his dad. He couldn't wait to tell him everything that had happened: how well he had played, how the Cyclones coach had been watching him, and what the coach had said to him after the game.

Jamal's dad was excited, too. He had played basketball as a young man. He had even gotten a scholarship to college before a knee injury ended his career.

He always wanted Jamal to play basketball and love it just as he had. But he never forced Jamal to play. Jamal's love for basketball was real.

Jamal told his dad the whole story. His dad agreed to drive him to the practice on Saturday so Jamal could try to make the team.

Finally, Jamal asked the big question that he had held inside through the whole story.

"Dad, can I get a pair of Show-25s for the tryout?" Jamal asked.

Jamal's father thought for a moment. "Now, what do you need new shoes for?" he said. "You managed to impress that coach wearing your old ones. Could be there's some magic in those shoes."

Jamal chuckled along with his dad.

He knew what his father was really saying. He didn't want to spend that much money on shoes. "But, Dad, those kids all have cool shoes," Jamal said. "These ratty old things will look stupid next to all those kids' shoes."

Jamal's father grew serious. "Now, son," he said. "Listen to me. You are who you are. You come from where you come from. You don't need to go buying any fancy shoes just to prove you belong."

Jamal's chin fell to his chest. "I know, Dad," he said. "I know." He had heard this speech many times before.

"Do you think those boys on the Cyclones are good players because of the shoes they wear?" Jamal's dad asked.

"No," Jamal said, guessing his dad's answer. "It's because they love the game and work hard."

"That's right," Jamal's dad said. "And you're a good player for the same reason."

Jamal had heard enough. "Never mind, Dad," he said. "It's okay. I'll wear my old shoes to the tryout."

They sat in silence for a moment. Finally, Jamal's dad spoke. "I'll make a deal with you," he said. "You wear your old shoes to the tryout. If you make the Cyclones, I'll buy you a brand-new pair of Show-25s."

Chapter 5

Jamal walked toward the gym doors at Westhaven Middle School.

His heart was in his throat. He wasn't sure he was going to be able to breathe. He had never been so nervous in his life.

The only thing making Jamal feel normal was the sound he heard in the distance. It was the sound of basketballs bouncing.

Jamal walked toward the noise.

When he reached the doors to the gym, he pulled them open slowly.

Inside, the bright lights of the gym lit up three full basketball courts. Each of them had regulation-sized glass backboards. The floor was freshly polished. Even the balls looked new.

All the players wore bright red warm-up pants and jackets as they shot around, getting ready for the start of practice.

Jamal stepped into the gym and the door slammed behind him.

Instantly, the gym fell silent.

All the boys turned and looked at Jamal. There was an uncomfortable pause. Then Jamal heard a friendly voice.

"Hey, everybody!" Coach Barker shouted. "Jamal's here!"

The boys returned quickly to their shooting and dribbling.

None of them stopped to say hi to Jamal.

Coach Barker trotted across the gym. "Hey, Jamal, I'm glad you came," he said. "This is going to be fun. I think you'll like these guys."

Jamal wasn't so sure.

"They don't seem all that excited to see me," he said.

"Ah, don't worry about that," the coach said. "They're like this with all the new kids. They'll get over it."

Jamal tried to smile.

He knew how to make himself feel comfortable. All he had to do was get a basketball in his hands.

Coach Barker directed him to the main court, and Jamal grabbed a ball and walked out.

He dribbled into the middle of the group, but he clearly didn't fit in. His worn shoes, black shorts, and white T-shirt stood out. All of the Cyclones looked so freshly pressed. Jamal didn't say a word, and no one spoke to him.

He lofted a short shot that swished through the net. "Oooh, he can shoot!" one boy whispered.

"Yeah, but he probably missed the clink of those metal nets on the playground," another shot back.

Jamal didn't even look. He just grabbed his ball, went out a little farther, and swished another shot.

A boy under that basket grabbed Jamal's ball and flipped it back to him.

"Nice shot," the boy said. Jamal glanced up, and they smiled at each other.

Coach Barker interrupted the warm-up with a sharp blast of his whistle. "Full-court fast-break drill!" he shouted.

All the players ran to different spots on the court to start the drill.

Jamal wasn't sure where to go, but he got in one of the lines anyway.

He watched the first couple of groups go, and instantly figured out what he was supposed to do.

When it was his turn, Jamal caught an outlet pass from a rebounder. He instantly dribbled to the middle of the court at full speed.

He had a player on each side of him. They were pushing up the court toward two defenders in a three-on-two drill.

Jamal darted up the floor. He made a little shoulder fake toward one of his teammates. The defender fell for it.

That left the lane wide open. Jamal cruised in for an easy layup.

"Hey, I was open!" called one of the boys.

Jamal ignored him. He hustled back on defense and helped stop the players who were trying to score on the other end.

It didn't take long for Jamal to prove that he was the best player on the court.

After fifteen minutes of the fast-break drill, Coach Barker called for a water break.

As the players walked to get some water, one of the boys bumped into Jamal. "You may make this team," he said, "but you'll never be one of us."

Suddenly, another boy grabbed him by the arm. It was the boy who passed the ball back to Jamal during warm-ups.

"Hey, listen," he said. "I'm Ricky. Just ignore Hank and those other guys. They hate everyone."

Jamal laughed. "Well, they sure don't like me," he said.

Practice continued for two hours. Jamal loved every minute of the basketball part. Getting to play on the gleaming courts with the best balls was a thrill.

He just didn't like the breaks in the action.

He got bored listening to the coach diagram plays. And he hated the awkward moments with the unfriendly players at the drinking fountain.

At the end of practice, Coach Barker walked over to Jamal. In front of the whole team, he said, "I want you all to welcome the newest Cyclone to the team!"

No one cheered. Ricky walked up and bumped fists with Jamal, but he was alone.

Chapter 6

Special Surprise

When Jamal walked out of the gym, his dad was waiting for him in the car. Next to him on the front seat was a plastic bag. It said "Fleet Feet" on the side.

Jamal opened the door and jumped in. He saw the bag and opened it up, pulling out the shoebox. Inside was a pair of Show-25s, just his size.

"Dad!" he yelped. "How did you know I'd make the team?"

His dad smiled. "Was there ever any doubt?"

They smiled at each other. On the ride home, however, Jamal's face changed. He wasn't sure that he really wanted to play for the Cyclones. Other than Ricky, the boys on the team didn't seem to want him around.

Jamal knew he was a good player. He was good enough to play for the Cyclones, but he wondered if he'd really like it that much.

He didn't have that much time to think about it.

The next practice was in two days. The first games were coming up in less than a week. Jamal would have to study hard to learn the team's plays.

But first came Sunday. That meant another full day of playing ball on the playground.

Jamal and Michael went down to the playground to get in some pickup games.

Michael was excited that Jamal had made the Cyclones.

"I can't believe that one of us is playing on that awesome team!" he kept saying over and over.

Jamal was worried about what the other kids might think. He wondered if they would still accept him.

He didn't have to wait long for an answer.

When Jamal got to the playground, the game that was going on stopped.

All of the older boys on the court just stood there, staring at Jamal.

They looked angry. Nobody moved.

It seemed like an eternity.

What's going on? Jamal thought. Don't they want me around here any more?

Just then, all of the players started laughing.

"Man, we're just playing with you!" one of them shouted. Then all of the boys ran over to Jamal. They started giving him high fives and chest bumps.

Jamal felt better. He knew he'd always have a home on the playground.

* * *

Monday night, it was time for his first "real" practice with the Cyclones.

Jamal threw his Show-25s into his bag and hopped in the car. When he got to the gym, he quickly put on his new shoes. Then he headed out onto the court.

The shoes felt great. Almost too great, in fact. They were cushioned on the inside and much softer than Jamal was used to. Still, they looked and felt fantastic.

"Hey!" Hank shouted to the group. "Looks like somebody scraped up enough money for some new shoes! Or did you steal those?"

Jamal didn't flinch.

He knew what Hank was doing. He was trying to get him mad so he'd do something stupid.

Jamal just grabbed a ball and trotted out to the court.

Coach Barker didn't hear the comment. He blew his whistle to start practice.

"Boys, we've only got a couple of practices before our first games this weekend," Coach Barker said. "We're going to have to concentrate and work hard this week. Now let's go."

The boys started doing the fast-break drill. However, the first time the ball was passed to Jamal, it slipped through his fingers.

Jamal recovered and sprinted up court with the ball. He faked to his right and passed the ball toward Ricky, who was on his left. But the pass was way too high. It sailed out of bounds.

Throughout the whole practice, Jamal couldn't do anything right.

Jamal nodded. But when he went back out on the court, nothing was different. At the very end of practice, he tried to throw a lob pass to a teammate. The pass was so bad it banged off the wall at the end of the gym. When practice ended, Jamal ran out of the gym.

He didn't say a word the whole ride home. When he got to his bedroom, he ripped the Show-25s out of his bag and threw them against his bedroom wall.

The first game was the next day, and he didn't know what to do.

When Jamal arrived at the gym for the first game, he sat down on the floor to put on his shoes. But when he reached into the bag, they were gone.

All he had were his ratty old shoes.

His shots clanged off the rim. His passes got stolen or went out of bounds. He even dribbled the ball off his own foot once. It was a complete nightmare.

When practice finally ended, Jamal knew what he'd hear.

Sure enough, Hank walked over to him. "Nice practice," Hank said sarcastically. "Have you played this game before?"

Chapter 7

The rest of the week was much of the same. Jamal kept finding himself in the wrong place on the court, doing the wrong thing. He struggled to make any shots. His passes didn't reach anyone.

On defense, it wasn't much better. He was being beaten by players he knew he could guard.

His relationships with the other Cyclones weren't getting any better, either.

Ricky was being nice, but the other kids on the team were not. Sometimes they would laugh at his mistakes. Sometimes they would get angry.

Finally, during the last practice, Hank went up to Coach Barker. "You're not actually going to let this kid play in the games, are you?" he said. "He's terrible."

"That's enough, Hank," Coach Barker said. "Jamal needs our support."

Coach Barker decided it was time to pull Jamal aside.

"Look, Jamal," he said. "I know you're having a tough time. I think you're just trying too hard. On the playground, you just relax and play. Here, it seems like you're thinking too much and not just playing the game."

He didn't know what to do. His new shoes were sitting on the floor of his bedroom. His old shoes would look awful with the brand-new Cyclones uniform. But he didn't really have a choice. He had to put them on.

During warm-ups, Hank and some of the other Cyclones made fun of his shoes. Jamal tried to ignore them. He was more worried about how well he would play in the game. He was worried that the coach might not play him at all.

As the clock wound down on pregame warm-ups, Coach Barker called the players over to the bench. "Okay," he said. "Here's how we're going to start. Hank, you'll start at center. Ricky and Mark, you'll be the forwards. Darius, you will be the two-guard. Jamal, you'll start at point guard."

Hank looked shocked. Jamal was starting! Ricky was smiling. Jamal didn't know what to do or say.

The coach sent the boys out onto the floor. Jamal stared at his shoes. Out of all ten players on the court, his shoes were the oldest. Everyone else had brand-new shoes.

The players shook hands and the referee tossed the ball up.

Hank won the jump, tipping it to Ricky.

Ricky quickly threw the ball to Jamal.

The instant the ball hit his hands, Jamal felt different. Jamal raced through the other team, darting to the basket for an easy layup.

Back at the other end, Jamal crouched low on defense.

He watched his player dribble. At just the right moment, Jamal reached in and tipped the ball away. He sprinted to the other end and made another easy layup.

Before long, the Cyclones were in control. Jamal was feeding his teammates easy baskets, and the Cyclones built a lead of 22–6. Finally, Coach Barker took the starters out for a rest. On the bench, Hank sat down next to Jamal.

Jamal sat there, staring at his old shoes. Maybe my dad was right, he thought. Maybe these shoes do have some magic in them.

The Cyclones finished that first game off easily with a win. Jamal played great the entire game. He led the team in scoring, and he also had the most assists. It was a great start to the season.

Chapter 8

Turnaround

Jamal made a decision. He was going to wear his old shoes for the rest of the season.

His father wasn't too happy about it, because the Show-25s were expensive. Jamal brought the newer shoes to every game, but he couldn't bring himself to put them on.

The season passed by quickly. Jamal led the Cyclones to twenty-six wins and only two losses during the regular season.

Hank and the other boys still didn't talk much to him, but at least they stopped making fun of him. Meanwhile, Ricky was becoming one of his best friends.

The Cyclones breezed through the first three rounds of the state playoffs. They won each game easily.

Finally, it was time for the championship game. Jamal had never been so excited to play a game in his life.

When the Cyclones took the court, Jamal had a big surprise waiting for him.

His father was there, as he always was for Jamal's games. But this time, he brought Jamal's older brother and Michael along. Most of the high-school boys from the neighborhood had come to watch the game, too.

The big crowd didn't make Jamal nervous. If anything, it made him more fired up to play.

The Cyclones were playing a team called the Spartans. They were a big, strong team, and one of only two teams to beat the Cyclones during the regular season. Jamal had played well that game, but he knew he'd have to play even better for the Cyclones to win the title.

When the referee tossed the ball up, Hank leaped for it and tapped it to Jamal. Without hesitation, Jamal fired the ball up court to Ricky. Ricky caught it in the lane and made the easy layup. The Cyclones were off to a fast start!

The Spartans were tough, and the first half of the game was very tight.

The Spartans had one great outside shooter who made four three-pointers. With a minute left in the first half, the Spartans were leading, 32–31.

The Cyclones had the ball, and Coach Barker told Jamal to stall and set up for one last shot in the half.

Jamal followed the instructions. He dribbled above the three-point line until there were eight seconds left on the clock. Then he quickly fired a pass to Ricky on the wing. Jamal cut behind his player and down the lane. Ricky returned the pass. Jamal made one dribble, but was cut off in the lane by a Spartans player.

That left Hank open, and Jamal spun and fed him with a pass. Hank caught it and laid it in the basket just before the buzzer sounded.

After Jamal let go of the pass, he tripped over something and fell. When Hank's layup dropped in the basket, Jamal was laying on the ground.

As the other players celebrated and started toward the bench, Ricky went to help Jamal up. But Jamal just sat there, staring at his right shoe.

The sole had finally worn down and had ripped off the bottom of the shoe. Jamal's magic shoes were wrecked.

Ricky helped him up. Jamal held the torn sole in his hands as he walked off the court. "It's okay," Ricky said. "You've got your new shoes with you, right?"

"Yeah," Jamal said. "But these shoes were magic."

"Magic?" Ricky said. "Are you serious?"

Jamal reminded Ricky of how badly he had played in practice with the new shoes on.

Ricky just shook his head. Coach Barker gave the boys some halftime instructions. Jamal reluctantly put his new shoes on.

Hank saw the look on Jamal's face. "What's your problem?" he muttered. "Can't you play in real basketball shoes?"

Instantly, Jamal's head popped up. He stared back at Hank, not saying a word.

The Cyclones got the ball first, and Ricky passed it in to Jamal.

The ball bounced off his fingers and hit the floor.

A Spartan player lunged for it, but Jamal pulled it back in. With a nifty spin move, he got away.

He moved the ball up the court and lofted a lob pass toward Hank.

It was a beautiful play. The ball settled into Hank's hands. He made a quick fake and then banked in a short shot.

Jamal heard a cry from the sideline: "Oh, yeah!" It was Michael. "There's more of that coming your way!"

In an instant, Jamal felt a tingle all over his body. The butterflies were gone. All that was left was energy.

In the second half, the Spartans were no match for the Cyclones. Jamal led the way, driving for layups, dishing out assists, and stealing the ball.

When the final horn sounded, the Cyclones had won, 62–51.

The players whooped it up on the court.

They jumped into each other's arms and high-fived. Michael came down on the court and wrapped Jamal in a big hug.

Finally, Hank walked over to Jamal and offered his hand. "Good season," he said. "I guess you're a real Cyclone now."

Jamal nodded. "But I'm still a boy from the neighborhood," Jamal said, smiling. "That isn't changing."

The next morning, Jamal and Michael went to the playground to play ball. Ricky arranged to meet them there.

Jamal wore his Show-25s.

But his worn-out old shoes were still in his bag.

ABOUT THE AUTHOR

Bob Temple lives in Rosemount, Minnesota, with his wife and three children. He has written more than thirty books for children. Over the years, he has coached more than twenty kids' soccer, basketball, and baseball teams. He also loves visiting classrooms to talk about his writing.

ABOUT THE ILLUSTRATOR

When Sean Tiffany was growing up, he lived on a small island off the coast of Maine. Every day, from sixth grade until he graduated from high school, he had to take a boat to get to school. When Sean isn't working on his art, he works on a multimedia project called "OilCan Drive," which combines music and art. He has a pet cactus named Jim.

GLOSSARY

assist (uh-SIST)—a basketball play in which one player helps a teammate score

backboard (BAK-bord)—the hard surface behind a basketball net

dribble (DRIB-uhl)—to bounce a basketball while keeping it under your control

drill (DRIL)—the act of practicing a skill over and over again

layup (LAY-up)—a basketball shot in which a player shoots the ball from very close to the basket

playoff (PLAY-awf)—a game or series of games played after the regular season to help determine a champion

point guard (POYNT GARD)—the player on a basketball team who handles the ball the most and sets up the team's offensive plays

showboat (SHOH-boht)—to show off your skills in a way that calls attention to yourself

FROM THE PLAYGROUND

Many of the best players ever to play basketball have played on public courts and playgrounds in America's largest cities. In fact, many of the top stars in the NBA first gained fame playing on the playgrounds in cities like New York and Chicago.

Players like Connie Hawkins, Lew Alcindor (who later became known as Kareem Abdul-Jabbar), and Stephon Marbury were playground legends long before they became NBA superstars.

But many of the best playground players never made it to the NBA. One of the best playground players ever was a man named Earl "The Goat" Manigault. He wasn't particularly tall at just over six feet, but during the 1960s, he was a terror on the court.

TO THE MAJOR LEAGUES

His leaping ability was also legendary. He could dunk with either hand, and it's been said that he could grab a quarter off the top of a backboard.

In the summers, many of the pro players would return to New York City and play in the Rucker League with many of the best playground players. Even the best NBA players couldn't stop him.

Sadly, Manigault never played in the NBA or even college basketball because his drug use got in the way. But after spending time in prison, Manigault devoted his life to helping kids stay in school and stay away from drugs.

DISCUSSION QUESTIONS

1. Why do you think Jamal was worried that his friends at the playground court would stop liking him after he made the Cyclones?

2. When Hank made fun of Jamal, Jamal never reacted to him. What do you think Jamal was feeling when Hank did that?

3. Even though Hank was mean to him, Jamal kept passing him the ball. Why do you think he did that?

4. When Jamal's shoe broke, what do you think he was feeling?

WRITING PROMPTS

1. Have you ever had a lucky item of clothing that you wore? Write about it and the good luck you felt that it brought you.

2. Have you ever had to fit in with people who weren't like you? Write about that experience.

3. Did you ever try out for a sports team or other organization? Write about what it was like.

JAKE MADDOX

SNOWBOARD DUEL

STONE ARCH *Realistic Fiction*

Hannah and Brian have the run of Snowstream, a cool winter resort. But a new kid, Zach, starts a boys-only snowboard cross team. What will Brian do when he's forced to choose between Hannah and snowboarding?

BY JAKE MADDOX

JAKE MADDOX

SOCCER SHOOTOUT

STONE ARCH *Realistic Fiction*

Berk always plays goalie for his soccer team. But when a new kid, Ryan, moves to town, Berk has to play an unfamiliar position. Ryan may have incredible talent, but he's also wildly unpredictable. Can the team survive the season?